Printed in Great Britain
for J.M. Dent & Sons Ltd
91 Clapham High Street
London SW4 7TA

Dent
Children's
Books
LONDON

A Pocketbook of Painful Puns and Poems

by Jonathan Allen

The Whooping Bear

The Whooping Bear
   Has long curly hair
Which he ties up in bunches with ribbon,
   He welcomes the day
   With a tremulous neigh
Similar to that of the gibbon.

The Whooping Bear
   Has long curly hair
But his children are stripey and dotted,
   They jump and they shout,
   Whilst juggling with trout,
Which are afterwards pickled and potted.

Puns

Growing a Little Horse

Window Pain

A Burglar Making off with his Lute

Bedside Manor

A Belt round the Ear

Fifty Strokes of the Cat

A Social Climber

Lancing a Boil

Misspellings

Camels are mainly found in the dessert

Diary Farming

Newly Hatched Chic

Hairs on your chess

Being soundly
Frogged

A bottle of Mousewash

Nursing a Broken Hearth

A Badger Celebrates

A Badger always celebrates
    His birthday on the proper date,
He leaps out from his burrow
    With a massive birthday grin,

Turns somersaults of pleasure,
Gives three cheers for good measure,

Then reads through all
his birthday cards,

And smiling, jumps

back

in

Puns

The Seal of Approval

A Grave Face

Painting a Freeze on the Wall

Lambs Gambling in the Fields

Chain Mail

Officers' Mess

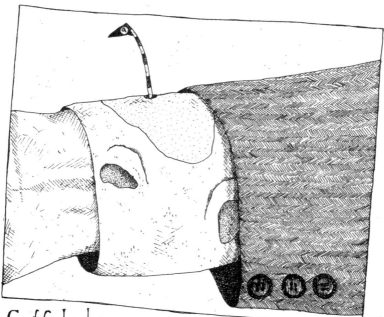

Cuff-Links

Cuff Lynx

Names

Ed was a Wapiti
  Dealing in property,
Joe was an Owl
  With a bag on his head,

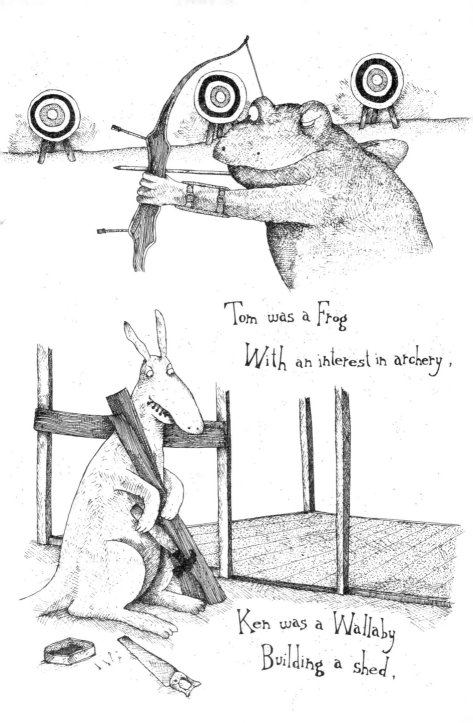

Tom was a Frog
With an interest in archery,

Ken was a Wallaby
Building a shed,

Jim was an Eagle
Who wallowed in treacle,

Bill was a Marmot
Who played the bassoon,

Geoff was a Stoat
With a flourishing
Fish business,

Ben was a Wombat
Who flew to the Moon.

The enterprise shown by these creatures
should be
A valuable lesson to you
and to me.

Misspellings

A holiday in Grease

A Duke Box

Lunching a Ship

The long arm of the Lawn

A Leek in the Pipes

Lost in the Maize

Chocolate Moose

A Hot-Air Baboon

Things I have not Seen

I have seen many things
And done many deeds,
But I've not seen an Antelope
Covered in beads.

I've been to the Tropics
I've been to the Poles,
But I've never seen Elephants
Living in holes.

I have lived with Hamsters
And dwelt with Newts,
But I've not seen a Chicken
In thigh-length boots.

Though I've travelled the World
Observing it all ,
I've not seen an Aardvark
Fifty feet tall .

From African jungles
To bleak northern wastes,
I've not seen a Stoat
With a smile on its face.

From the highest of heights
To the deepest of seas,
I've never seen Buffalo
Swinging from trees.

From hottest desert
To coldest ice,
I've never had hand luggage
Stolen by Mice.

Though strange and exciting
My travels have been,
They still leave me yearning
For things yet unseen.

Clichés

He's got his Father's nose

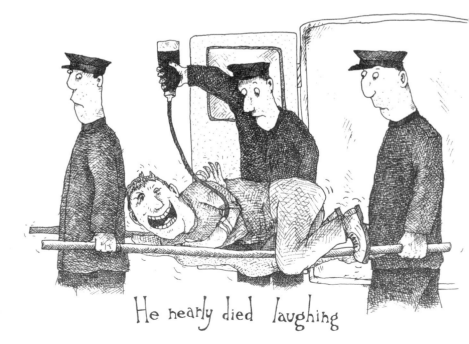

He nearly died laughing

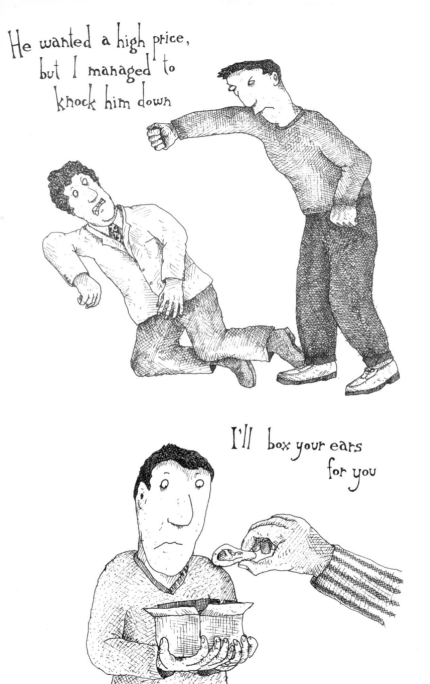

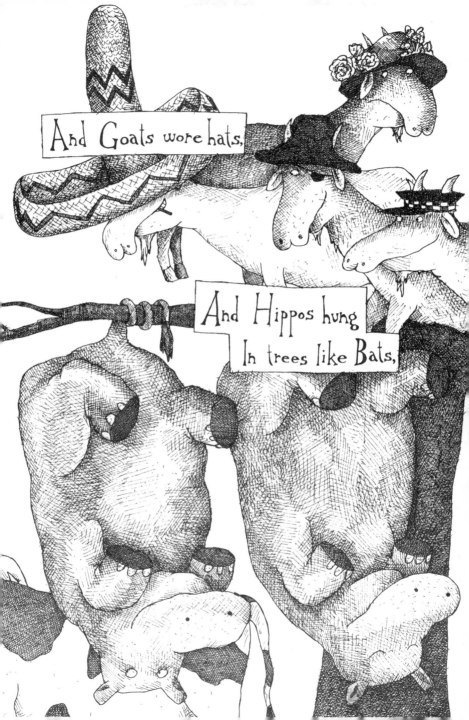

And Goats wore hats,

And Hippos hung
In trees like Bats,

The Lurking Horror

It lurks inside pianos,   It waits for your mistakes,

A clumsy discord renders it   immediately awake,

Then,

bursting from its hiding place,   With fearsome fangs and eyes,

Comes a toad of cruel aspect,   A toad of nightmare size,

To punish you for playing
B flat ninth instead of C,
And singing in the key of F
Whilst playing tunes in D.

Misspellings

Fish and Chimps

A Group of Close Fiends

Rhyming Moles

A Rock n' Roll Mole

A Mole in a Bowl

A going-for-a-Stroll Mole

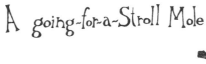

A Droll Mole

A Mole up a Pole

An out-on-Parole Mole

A hard-to-Console Mole

An out-of-Control Mole

A Toll Mole

A Tyrol Mole

A dramatic Rôle Mole

A scoring-a-Goal Mole

Puns

An Urban Gorilla

House Hunting

A Bore Hole

A Nice Little Tramp in the Woods

A Small Hamlet

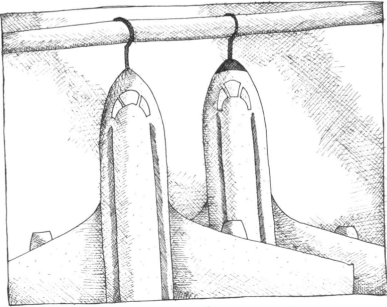

Aircraft Hanger

Shopping List

Dove Coat

Pirate Song

Paint me legs with yoghurt, lads!
The tide is nearly high,
Stick a lupin in me hat
And poke me in the eye,
For I must sail the seas, me lads
A pirate captain bold,
I must sail the seven seas
In search of pirate gold.

The monkey's in the cupboard lads!
The wind is in the west,
Stuff a rabbit down me boot
And go and wash me vest,
For I must sail the seas, me lads
A pirate captain strong,
I must sail the seven seas
And sing a pirate song.

Go and fetch a wardrobe lads!
And fill it full of cheese,
Wash me budgie down the sink
And grasp me by the knees,
For I must sail the seas, me lads,
A pirate captain feared,
I must sail the seven seas
And grow a pirate beard.

Pelt me with bananas lads!
The wind is in the east,
Help me shave this kangaroo
And fill it s ears with yeast,
For I must sail the seas me lads
A pirate captain brave,
I must sail the seven seas
'Till I die in a pirate grave!

Wombat

Oh Wombat, Wombat!
So deadly in combat,
So brave and so handsome
So fierce and so free,

Your enemies fear you
They dare not come near you
No matter how cunning
Or bad they might be.